If you call upon them, ring the b
Three times twice.

The name of their house I cannot tell
But they've learnt a trade and are doing well

Three Proud Mice
Three Proud Mice
   Soon settled down
   Soon settled down.

And soon their tails began to grow,
And their eyes recovered their sight, you know;
They looked in the glass and it told them so,
These three Wise Mice.

Three Wise Mice
Three Wise Mice
    Rubbed rubbed away
    Rubbed rubbed away,

They sought a Chemist and found a Friend;
He gave them some "Never too late to mend"
These three Sick Mice.

Three Sick Mice
Three Sick Mice
    Gave way to tears
    Gave way to tears.
They could not see and they had no end;

Did you ever see such a sight in your life
As three Blind Mice?

Who cut off their tails with the carving knife.

They all ran after the Farmer's Wife,

Three Blind Mice
Three Blind Mice

See how they run
See how they run.

The bramble hedge was most unkind:
It scratched their eyes and made them blind,
And soon each Mouse went out of his mind,
These three Sad Mice.

So they hid themselves in the bramble hedge,
These three Scared Mice.

Three Sad Mice
Three Sad Mice
What could they do?
What could they do?

They jumped out onto the window ledge;
The mention of "Cat" set their teeth on edge;

Three Scared Mice
Three Scared Mice

Ran for their lives
Ran for their lives.

Just wait a minute: I'll fetch the Cat."
Oh dear! Poor Mice.

Three Poor Mice
Three Poor Mice
Soon changed their tone
Soon changed their tone.

The Farmer's Wife said, "What are you at,
And why were you capering round like that?

They felt so happy they danced with glee;
But the Farmer's Wife came in to see
What might this merrymaking be
Of three Glad Mice.

Three Glad Mice
Three Glad Mice
Ate all they could
Ate all they could.

The Farmer was eating some bread and cheese;
So they all went down on their hands and knees,
And squeaked, "Pray give us a morsel, please,"
These three Starved Mice.

Three Starved Mice
Three Starved Mice

Came to a Farm
Came to a Farm.

Three Hungry Mice
Three Hungry Mice
　　Searched for some food
　　Searched for some food.

But all they found was a walnut shell
That lay by the side of a dried-up well;
Who had eaten the nut they could not tell,
These three Hungry Mice.

Three Cold Mice
Three Cold Mice
    Woke up next morn
    Woke up next morn.

They each had a cold and a swollen face,
Through sleeping all night in an open space;
So they rose quite early and left the place,
These three Cold Mice.

So they all slept out in a field instead,
These three Bold Mice.

Three Bold Mice
Three Bold Mice
  Came to an Inn
  Came to an Inn.

"Good evening, Host, can you give us a bed?"
But the Host he grinned and he shook his head

And all the luggage they took was a comb,
These three Small Mice.

They made up their minds to set out to roam;
Said they, "'Tis dull to remain at home,"

Three Small Mice
Three Small Mice
    Pined for some fun
    Pined for some fun.

THREE BLIND MICE

For Scotty, Kevin, Clive

and Edward who is the big cheese

BOOKS ILLUSTRATED BY VICTORIA CHESS

Jim, Who Ran Away from His Nurse, and Was Eaten by a Lion

A Little Touch of Monster

Slugs

Three Blind Mice

Illustrations copyright © 1990 by Victoria Chess

Musical arrangement © 1985 by Grand Trunk Music,
reprinted by permission from *Sharon, Lois & Bram's Mother Goose.*

First edition
Library of Congress Cataloging-in-Publication Data

Ivimey, John W. (John William), b. 1868.
The complete story of the three blind mice / by John W. Ivimey;
illustrated by Victoria Chess.
p.   cm.
Originally published: Complete version of ye three blind mice.
Summary: Three small mice in search of fun become hungry, scared,
blind, wise, and finally happy.
ISBN 0-316-13867-3
[1. Mice—Fiction. 2. Stories in rhyme.] I. Chess, Victoria,
ill. II. Title. III. Title: Three blind mice.
PZ8.3.I83Co   1989   88-1302
[E]—dc 19   CIP
                                                    AC

Joy Street Books are published by Little, Brown and
Company (Inc.)

10 9 8 7 6 5 4 3 2 1

HR

Designed by Sara Reynolds

Published simultaneously in Canada by
Little, Brown & Company (Canada) Limited
Printed in the United States of America

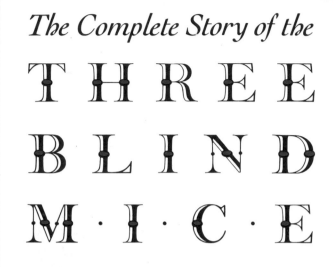

The Complete Story of the

THREE
BLIND
M·I·C·E

by John W. Ivimey

illustrated by
Victoria Chess

Joy Street Books

Little, Brown and Company
BOSTON   TORONTO   LONDON